# KATIE WOO

## Celebrates

by Fran Manushkin
illustrated by Tammie Lyon

capstone

Katie Woo is published by Picture Window Books
A Capstone Imprint
1710 Roe Crest Drive
North Mankato, MN 56003
www.capstonepub.com

Text © 2013 Fran Manushkin
Illustrations © 2013 Picture Window Books

Library of Congress Cataloging-in-Publication Data
Manushkin, Fran.
  Katie Woo celebrates / by Fran Manushkin; illustrated by Tammie Lyon.
    p. cm. -- (Katie Woo)
Summary: In these four previously published stories, Katie celebrates Valentine's Day, the Fourth of July, Halloween, and Thanksgiving with her friends.
ISBN 978-1-4048-8100-6 (pbk.)
1. Woo, Katie (Fictitious character)—Juvenile fiction. 2. Chinese Americans—Juvenile fiction. 3. Holidays—Juvenile fiction. 4. Friendship—Juvenile fiction. [1. Chinese Americans—Fiction. 2. Holidays—Fiction. 3. Friendship—Fiction.] I. Lyon, Tammie, ill. II. Title. III. Series: Manushkin, Fran. Katie Woo.
  PZ7.M3195Kbf 2013
  813.54—dc23                                        2012029151

Photo Credits
Greg Holch, pg. 96; Tammie Lyon, pg. 96

Designer: Kristi Carlson

Printed in the United States of America in Stevens Point, Wisconsin.
112012    007047R

# Table of Contents

# No Valentines for Katie

It was a cold gray day, but Katie was happy. It was Valentine's Day!

At school, Miss Winkle said, "Let's start the day with a valentine math puzzle."

"Take out your crayons, and draw a big heart. Then try to guess how many candy hearts will fit inside of it."

Katie drew a big red heart. Then she looked at the tiny candy hearts.

One said, "Puppy Love." Another said, "Melt My Heart."

"I think this heart will hold twelve candies," Katie decided. But when she filled up the heart, it held twenty.

"Boy, did I guess wrong!" Katie said.

"I love these tiny hearts," she said, smiling.

She couldn't stop reading them. She read "Cloud Nine" and "Soul Mate."

Miss Winkle said, "Now print your name on a piece of paper, and put it in the valentine box."

Then the class went out for recess.

When they came back, Miss
Winkle said, "Now the real fun starts!"

"Take out a piece of paper from the valentine box. You will make a valentine for the person that you pick," said Miss Winkle.

Katie picked Barry, the new boy.
As Katie began painting, Miss
Winkle said, "Each valentine should
say something nice about the person."

Katie whispered to JoJo, "I wonder who made me a valentine? I can't wait to see what it says about me!"

Ella read her card first. "This valentine is for Pedro. I like you because you are a great goalie! When we play soccer, you know how to use your head!"

"Thanks!" Pedro said.

Charlotte read her valentine. "JoJo, I like you because you jump rope so fast! And when I forget to bring my lunch, you share yours with me."

"Thank you!" said JoJo, beaming.

One by one, the students read their valentines. But nobody read one for Katie.

Katie's eyes filled with tears. "Someone got my name," she said, "but I guess they couldn't think of anything nice to say. That's why I didn't get a card."

"Katie," said Miss Winkle, "are you
sure you put your name into the box?"

"Oh, no!" Katie groaned. "I forgot!
I was so busy reading my candy
hearts."

"Well," said Miss Winkle, "since Katie did not get a card, will someone come up to the board and write something nice about her?"

"I will!" said Barry, the new boy.

He wrote, "I think Katie is very funny. And her glasses are just like mine!"

Katie smiled. "Thank you!" she said.

Now Barry looked sad. "I didn't get a card," he said.

Katie jumped up. "I got your name!" she said.

"Barry, I don't know you very well, but I think you are funny! Plus you have the same glasses as me!"

Barry couldn't stop smiling. "Katie, we said the same things!"

After school, Katie said, "Barry, can you walk home with us?"

"Sure," he agreed. "Do you promise to be funny?"

"I always am!" said Katie.

And they laughed together all the way home.

# Red, White, and Blue, and Katie Woo!

"The Fourth of July is my favorite holiday!" said Katie Woo.

JoJo laughed. "Katie, you say that about every holiday!"

"I guess I do," Katie said with a smile. "But the Fourth of July is the best! We're having a parade and a party in my backyard."

"And don't forget the fireworks," said Pedro.

Katie and Pedro and JoJo put red, white, and blue decorations on their bikes.

Everyone cheered when they rode by in the parade.

"Way to go!" yelled Katie's mom and dad.

After the parade, they went back to Katie's house. Pedro said, "Katie, your yard is so big, we can play soccer in it."

Katie kicked the ball hard.

"I can get it!" yelled Pedro. He backed up to hit the ball with his head.

Oops! Pedro tripped over the table and fell down. He spilled cherry soda all over his head!

"No points for you!" yelled Katie Woo.

"The hot dogs are ready," called
her dad. "Where are the buns?"

"Uh-oh!" Katie groaned. "JoJo's dog ate them!"

The hot dogs looked lonely without buns.

Katie's mom put out big bowls
of strawberries and blueberries and
whipped cream.

"We'll eat this later," she said. "It
will be our dessert."

"I'd like to eat it now," said JoJo.

"Come on," Katie said. "Let's play ringtoss."

The three friends tossed red, white, and blue hoops at stakes in the ground.

"I keep missing!" said JoJo. She cheered herself up by eating a few blueberries. Whenever she missed, JoJo ate some more.

Pedro won the ringtoss game.

"Uh-oh," JoJo groaned. "I think
I ate too many blueberries. I have a
stomachache."

Then it began to rain!

"Oh, no!" Katie groaned. "No fireworks!"

They began bringing all the food inside.

Katie carried the whipped cream.

"I'd like a little taste," Katie decided. She pressed the button hard — too hard!

Whipped cream sprayed everywhere! JoJo's dog licked it up.

"Our Fourth of July party is truly red, white, and blue," said Katie. "Pedro turned red when he spilled cherry soda on his head. I am white because I'm covered with whipped cream."

"And I felt blue," said JoJo, "from
eating too many blueberries."

"Look," said Pedro, "the rain stopped."

"Yay!" cheered Katie. "There will be fireworks!"

"First, let's have dessert," said
Katie's mom.

"I'll skip the blueberries," decided
JoJo.

The three friends sat together in the backyard.

"What color will the fireworks be?" asked Pedro.

"Red, white, and blue!" said Katie.

And she was right.

# Boo, Katie Woo!

Halloween was coming.

Katie asked Pedro and JoJo,
"What are you going to be?"

"I'm going to be a cowgirl," said JoJo.

"I'm going to be a magician," said Pedro. "What are you going to be, Katie?"

"A monster!" shouted Katie. "I'll scare everyone silly!"

Finally, it was Halloween!

Katie, Pedro, and JoJo went trick-or-treating together.

Katie rang the first bell.

A girl answered.

"Boo!" shouted Katie Woo.

The girl laughed. "You don't scare
me!" she said.

"I can do a trick!" said JoJo.

She twirled her cowgirl rope and jumped in and out of it.

"Cool!" said the
girl. She gave JoJo
lots of candy.

Katie, Pedro, and JoJo went to the
next house. A boy answered this time.

"Boo!" shouted Katie Woo.

"You don't scare me!" said the boy.

"I can do a magic trick," said Pedro.

He made a spoon bend by just looking at it!

"Cool trick!" The boy smiled. He gave Pedro a lot of candy.

As they walked to the next house, their friend Jake came running by.

"Have you seen a little brown kitten?" he asked. "She ran away, and I can't find her."

"We haven't," said Katie. "I'm sorry."

Just then, the three friends heard a spooky shriek!

"Yikes!" yelled JoJo.

"Don't be scared," said Katie. "It's only a squeaky gate swinging in the wind."

As they walked along, Katie said, "I'm not having any fun. I haven't scared anyone."

At the next house, Katie yelled "BOO!" as loud as she could.

"Hi, Katie!" said Barry, a boy in her class. "I knew it was you!"

Katie was so mad, she stomped
her feet.

"Look!" said Pedro. "The moon
is out. It looks nice
and spooky."

"It's too spooky!" said JoJo with a
shiver.

"Yikes!" yelled Katie. "Something's
wiggling on the ground."

"It's a snake!" she screamed.

Katie climbed up a tree to get away.

"That's not a snake," said JoJo. "It's the shadow of my jump rope."

"Meow!" came a sound close to Katie in the tree.

"It's Jake's lost kitten," Katie said.
"It's a good thing I climbed this tree!"
"Don't be scared," Katie told the
kitten. "I'm going to take you home."

Jake hugged his kitten over and over. "How did you find her?" he asked.

Katie smiled. "Let's just say it was a trick that turned into a treat."

It was a very happy Halloween!

# Katie Saves Thanksgiving

It was Thanksgiving Day. Snow was falling. Lots and lots of snow.

"I can't wait for JoJo and Pedro to come over," said Katie. "This will be our first Thanksgiving together."

"I know a lot about the Pilgrims," Katie told her dad.

"Tell me about them," he said.

"It took a long time for the
Pilgrims to cross the sea," said Katie.
"And their ship, the *Mayflower*, went
through scary storms."

"JoJo and her family are driving through a snowstorm," said Katie. "I hope they don't get lost."

"Oh no!" said Katie's mom. "The stove isn't working!"

Katie's dad tried to fix it, but he couldn't.

"The Pilgrims had to eat cold food on the *Mayflower*," said Katie. "Their ship was made of wood. It could burn if they lit a fire."

"Maybe Pedro's family can bring some hot food," said Katie's mom.

She called them, but nobody was home.

"They must be on their way here," said Katie.

"I'll call JoJo," Katie said.

JoJo answered right away.

"Guess what?" said JoJo. "Our car is stuck in the snow! We're waiting for a tow truck."

"This is some Thanksgiving!" said Katie's dad when he heard the news.

"Without the stove, we cannot have sweet potatoes," said Katie's mom.

"Or pumpkin pie," her dad groaned.

"The snow is piling up," said
Katie's dad. "I'd better go shovel it."
"I'll help you," said Katie.

Katie and her dad began to shovel.

"Mrs. West lives alone," said Katie.

"I'll shovel her sidewalk for her."

After a while, Mrs. West called
out, "Katie, thank you for your help.
Come inside. I made some hot cocoa."

Mrs. West's kitchen was filled with wonderful smells. "I made Thanksgiving dinner for my family," she said.

Just then her phone rang. As Mrs. West listened, her face grew sadder and sadder.

She told Katie, "My family was going to take an airplane here. But it's a bad day for flying. I guess I will be eating all alone."

Katie looked out the window. She
saw JoJo and Pedro.

Katie said, "Mrs. West, why don't
you come over and eat with us?"

"What a wonderful idea!" said
Mrs. West.

"Um," said Katie, "could you bring
your turkey and sweet potatoes? Our
stove isn't working."

"I would love to!" said Mrs. West.

Katie and JoJo and Pedro helped
Mrs. West carry the food to Katie's
house.

"This is just like the first Thanksgiving," said Katie. "The Pilgrims and the Indians shared their food, too."

"But they didn't have my pumpkin pie," said Mrs. West.

"But WE do!" said Katie.

Everyone was very thankful!

# Cooking with Katie Woo!

## Behold-My-Heart Breadsticks

*Makes 12 breadsticks

Valentine's Day is the perfect day to cook something special for the people you love. Here is an easy recipe that will go with any Valentine's Day dinner. Before you get started, ask a grown-up for help, and don't forget to wash your hands!

### Ingredients:

- 1 can of refrigerated breadsticks
- 1 egg, beaten
- 2 tablespoons Parmesan cheese

### Other things you need:

- a large cookie sheet
- a pastry brush
- a spoon

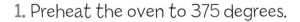

**What you do:**

1. Preheat the oven to 375 degrees.

2. Separate the breadstick dough into 12 pieces. Stretch each piece until it is 12 inches long.

3. Shape each piece into a heart. Pinch the ends together. Place the heart on the cookie sheet.

4. With the pastry brush, brush your hearts with the beaten egg.

5. With the spoon, shake a little Parmesan cheese on the top of each heart.

6. Bake for 10 to 13 minutes, or until golden brown. To make it extra yummy, try dipping your heart in warm pizza sauce. Enjoy!

# Pilgrim Pride Cookies

*Makes 24 cookies

Make a small Pilgrim hat that you can actually eat. It is the perfect Thanksgiving Day treat! Ask a grown-up for help, and be sure to wash your hands.

## Ingredients:

- 24 shortbread striped cookies
- 12-ounce bag of chocolate chips
- 24 marshmallows
- a tube of yellow decorator's frosting

## Other things you need:

- a cookie tray covered with waxed paper
- a medium microwave-safe bowl
- a large spoon
- toothpicks

## What you do:

1. Set the cookies with the striped-side down on the cookie tray. Space them apart.

2. Pour the chocolate chips in the bowl. Microwave for 1 minute. Stir with spoon. If the chips are not all melted, microwave an additional 30 seconds. Stir. Repeat until melted completely.

3. For each one, stick a toothpick into a marshmallow, dip it into the melted chocolate, and then center it on top of a cookie.

4. With a second toothpick, lightly hold down the marshmallow. Carefully pull out the first toothpick.

5. Chill until the chocolate sets. Then use the decorator's frosting to add a small rectangle on the marshmallow where it meets the cookie. It should look like the gold buckle on a Pilgrim's hat.

## About the Author

Fran Manushkin is the author of many popular picture books, including *Baby, Come Out!*; *Latkes and Applesauce: A Hanukkah Story*; *The Tushy Book*; *The Belly Book*; and *Big Girl Panties*. There is a real Katie Woo — she's Fran's great-niece — but she never gets in half the trouble of the Katie Woo in the books. Fran writes on her beloved Mac computer in New York City, without the help of her two naughty cats, Chaim and Goldy.

## About the Illustrator

Tammie Lyon began her love for drawing at a young age while sitting at the kitchen table with her dad. She continued her love of art and eventually attended the Columbus College of Art and Design, where she earned a bachelors degree in fine art. After a brief career as a professional ballet dancer, she decided to devote herself full time to illustration. Today she lives with her husband, Lee, in Cincinnati, Ohio. Her dogs, Gus and Dudley, keep her company as she works in her studio.